Para la niña más

Juguetona
I LOVE
YOU

ELISA

Published in the United States by Golden Books, an imprint of Random House Children's Books,
a division of Penguin Random House LLC, 1745 Broadway, New York, NY 10019, and in Canada
by Penguin Random House Canada Limited, Toronto, in conjunction with Disney Enterprises,
Inc. Golden Books, A Golden Book, A Big Golden Book, the G colophon, and the distinctive
gold spine are registered trademarks of Penguin Random House LLC.

randomhousekids.com

ISBN 978-0-7364-3506-2

Printed in the United States of America

10 9 8 7 6 5 4 3 2

Disney · PIXAR
FINDING DORY

Adapted by
Bill Scollon

Illustrated by
the Disney Storybook Art Team

g A GOLDEN BOOK • NEW YORK

Dory was a happy young fish. She lived in an underwater home with her parents, Jenny and Charlie. But Dory had one little problem. . . .

"Hi, I'm Dory. I suffer from short-term memory loss."

To help keep Dory safe, her parents taught her to tell others that she had a hard time remembering things.

One day, a strong current—an undertow—carried Dory far from home.

"Where are your parents?" asked a passing fish.

"I can't remember," replied Dory.

Dory told herself to **just keep swimming**. As the years went by, Dory forgot what she was looking for. . . .

Far out in the ocean, Dory met a clownfish named **Marlin**.
She helped him find his lost son, **Nemo**. Through their
adventures together, the fish became great friends.

Dory joined Marlin and Nemo in the coral reef and lived
next door to their anemone. Dory had a home again!
Marlin and Nemo loved Dory and kept her safe.

But one afternoon, a strong current spun Dory around and dropped her into the sand. She felt woozy and confused. "The Jewel of Morro Bay, California," she murmured.

When Dory felt better, Nemo told her what she had said.

All at once, memories came rushing back!

"I remember my family!" Dory shouted.

"We have to find them."

Dory, Marlin, and Nemo rode the ocean currents all the way to Morro Bay, California.

"Mom? Dad?" yelled Dory when they arrived.

Dory had been here before. She told some hermit crabs she was looking for her parents, two blue tangs named Jenny and Charlie.

"Jenny! Charlie!" cried Dory.

"SHHHHHH!"
said the hermit crabs.

A giant squid, bothered by all the yelling,
chased the three friends! They swam into
a kelp forest to escape.

Dory looked for someone who could help them. She heard a woman's voice above the water calling, "Won't you please join us?"

Marlin and Nemo followed Dory to the surface.

"Welcome to the Marine Life Institute," boomed the woman's voice through a speaker. "We believe in rescue, rehabilitation, and release."

Suddenly, **Dory was pulled out of the water!**

Dory was **tagged** and put in **Quarantine**, an area for sick or injured fish. She asked an octopus named Hank about the Jewel of Morro Bay.

"That's *this* place. The Marine Life Institute. You're here!" he said.

Hank noticed that Dory had a tag on her fin—and the tag meant she'd soon be transported to an aquarium in Cleveland! Hank desperately wanted to go there. Dory said she'd give him the tag if he helped her find her parents.

Hank took Dory to a **map of the exhibits**. Dory spotted a purple shell on the map. That brought back another memory.

Dory recalled lining up seashells with her parents. Her mom loved the purple ones.

"My home had a purple shell!"
she told Hank.

Moments later, a human carrying a bucket of fish came down the hall. Dory **leapt** into the bucket as Hank dashed out of sight.

DESTINY

Dory and Hank ended up in a pool with a whale shark named Destiny. The whale shark recognized Dory!

"We were pipe pals!" Destiny told Dory. They used to talk to each other through the pipes. Dory was from the Open Ocean exhibit.

"Can you take me there?" asked Dory.

Destiny said Dory could get there through the pipes. But Dory was worried that she'd get lost. Bailey, a beluga whale, could have guided her, but he said his echolocation wasn't working.

"There's no other way," said Hank.

Dory remembered her dad saying, **"There's always another way."** Then she spotted a stroller across from Destiny's pool. She had found another way!

Hank pushed the stroller while Dory navigated. But after a few wrong turns, Dory and Hank crashed into the touch pool. It was a nightmare! Little hands jabbed at them from every direction.

Dory remembered her parents saying,

"Just keep swimming!"

As Dory led Hank across the pool, somebody poked Hank and caused him to release his ink. The water turned **black** and scared all the kids away.

When Dory and Hank surfaced, they saw the Open Ocean exhibit. It was straight ahead!

ECHOLOCATION

THE WORLD'S MOST POWERFUL PAIR OF GLASSES

Meanwhile, Marlin and Nemo were trying
to get inside the Institute to find Dory. Luckily,
a loon named Becky agreed to fly them in.

**"Drop us
anywhere!"**
shouted Marlin.

Becky hung the bucket on a tree branch and swooped to the ground for a snack. The branch catapulted Marlin and Nemo into a small tank in the gift shop! Nothing was going right.

"What would Dory do?" they both asked.

The two clownfish noticed a line of jumping fountains across the plaza.

Without another thought, they leapt out of the tank and hopped along the jet streams!

At the same moment, Dory and Hank were at the top of the huge Open Ocean tank.

"Looks like this is it, kid," said Hank. "I have a truck to catch."

Dory handed him the tag. "You know, I think I'm going to remember you," she said. Then she swam off to find her family.

Dory followed a line of shells to her home. "Mom! Dad!" she yelled.
But no one was there.

Memories flooded back. Dory's parents had warned her about the
undertow. But one evening, she swam out to get a purple shell for her
mom. Dory went too close to the undertow and was pulled away!

Dory gasped.

"It was my fault.

My parents . . . I lost them."

A crab told Dory that all the blue tangs had been taken to Quarantine. "They're being shipped on a truck to Cleveland at the crack of dawn," he said.

Dory had to get back to Quarantine—fast!

"Go through the pipes," said another crab. "Two lefts and a right. Simple."

Dory bravely entered the maze of pipes, but she was soon lost. Then she remembered her pipe pal and called for help.

"Destiny!"

Destiny asked Bailey to try using his echolocation to help Dory. He sent out a call and listened for its echo.

Little by little, the pipes came into focus. "It's working!" Bailey shouted. Then he saw Dory. "Tell her to go left."

"OooOOOooo– OooOOoo."

But something else was in the pipes, too. And it was heading right for Dory!

Dory screamed!

"Oh no!" said Bailey. "It's eating her!"

"Oh, Dory!" Destiny sobbed.

But Dory couldn't have been happier. **It was Marlin and Nemo!**

"How did you two find me?" asked Dory.

"We were having a very hard time," said Marlin, "until Nemo asked, 'What would Dory do?'"

Dory, Marlin, and Nemo made it to the blue tang tank in
Quarantine. Dory's parents weren't there.

"They came here to look for you," said a fish. "But they never
came back. That was years ago."

Dory was stunned. "They're gone."

Just as the blue tangs were about to be loaded onto the truck
bound for Cleveland, Hank scooped up Dory. Then a human
grabbed Hank, causing him to drop her. She slipped
down a drain that led to the ocean!

Once again, Dory was alone. She felt hopeless. Then she remembered Nemo's words. "What would Dory do?"

Dory followed a path of shells. She saw two fish swimming toward her. **"Dory! You're here! You found us,"** said Jenny.

Her parents explained that when she'd gotten caught in the undertow, they went to look for her in Quarantine. When they didn't find her there, they went to search for her in the ocean.

"Have you been by yourself all these years?" asked Charlie.

Suddenly, Dory remembered Marlin and Nemo. She had to get them out of the blue tang tank and off that truck!

Dory and her parents swam to the surface just as the truck pulled away. She called to Destiny and Bailey, and they both jumped into the ocean to help!

Bailey used his echolocation.

"OooOOOooo."

The truck was heading for a bridge.

Dory needed a plan. She asked herself again, "What would Dory do?" When she saw a group of playful otters under the bridge, Dory had a plan!

The otters were happy to help. They climbed up to the road.
Then Destiny flipped Dory onto the highway. The otters caught
her, and on Dory's cue, they all embraced. Traffic came to a stop
as drivers admired the cuddly creatures.

One of the otters opened the back door of the truck
and brought Dory inside.

"You came back!" shouted Nemo.

"Of course," said Dory. **"You're family."**

Marlin called for Becky to fly them out of the truck.
But the loon flew off with only Marlin and Nemo. Dory
and Hank were still on their way to Cleveland!

Dory found another way out of the truck—through the skylight. Hank scared off the driver and grabbed the wheel. He put Dory in a cup on the dashboard.

"I steer, you navigate," said Hank.

The two friends turned the truck around and drove it into the ocean! Dory, her parents, Marlin, Nemo, Hank, Destiny, and Bailey were all reunited.

Not long after, everybody was living **happily together** in the coral reef.

Hank, Destiny, and Bailey enjoyed teaching at the school.

And Dory loved playing hide-and-seek with her parents,
just like they'd done when she was little. At last, surrounded
by her **family and friends**, Dory was truly home.

One day, Marlin followed Dory to the edge of the reef.
The two gazed out at the peaceful open ocean.

"**Wow**," said Marlin. "**It really is
quite a view.**"
Dory smiled.

"**Unforgettable.**"